S0-ASQ-235

CAN I KEEP HIM?

STORY AND PICTURES BY

STEVEN KELLOGG

DIAL BOOKS FOR YOUNG READERS

E. P. DUTTON, INC. ○ NEW YORK

86 03763

Library of Congress Catalog Card Number: 72-142453
Printed in the United States of America
Typography by Atha Tehon
COBE
15 14 13 12 11

FOR KEVIN

"Mom, I found this dog sitting all by himself. Can I keep him?"

"No, Arnold. Dogs are too noisy. He would bark all the time and annoy Mr. and Mrs. Van Doon next door. Take him back where you found him."

"I found a lost kitten wandering in the street. Can I keep him?"

"No, Arnold. Your grandma is allergic to cat fur. If we kept it, she couldn't visit anymore. Take him back where you found him, and please don't bring any more cats and dogs into the house."

"I found a shy fawn at the edge of the forest. He can't bark, and he doesn't have cat fur. Can I keep him?"

"No, dear. Fawns grow up to be wild bucks. They have sharp
hoofs and antlers. In one week our rugs and furniture would
be cut to bits."

"A funny little bear fell off a circus train. He wasn't hurt, and I brought him home. He can't bark, he has bear fur, and he has no hoofs. Can I keep him?"·

"No, dear. Bears have a disagreeable odor. The house will smell like a circus train."

"At the zoo Sweet Sally had three cubs. The zoo keeper said that the zoo only needs two more tigers, so he gave me one for a pet. He can't bark, he has tiger fur, his paws are soft, and he smells nice. Can I keep him?"

"No, dear. Tigers grow up to have terrible appetites. They eat enormous amounts of food, and sometimes they eat people. We could never afford to feed a tiger."

"A snake man at the carnival ran a contest to see who could guess how much the python weighs. I guessed right, and first prize was the snake. He makes no noise, he has no fur, he has no hoofs, he smells sweet, and he can go for a month without food. Can I keep him?"

"No, dear. Pythons are untidy reptiles. They slither around and shed their scaly skins all over the house. The skins clog the vacuum cleaner."

"In Alaska I saw a scientist chipping a dinosaur out of the
ice. When the dinosaur defrosted, he was still alive. The
museum didn't want a live dinosaur, so I brought him home.
He doesn't bark, he has no fur, he has big soft feet, he
doesn't shed—"

"Alaska? When were you ever in Alaska? And who ever
  heard of a dinosaur for a pet?"

"But I'm lonely. Will you play with me?"

"I'd like to, Arnold, but I'm busy. Why don't you run outside and
  play on the swing, or ride your bike, or dig in the sandbox?"

"He just moved in down the street. He doesn't bark, he has no fur, he has no hoofs, he smells like us, he doesn't eat much, he doesn't shed, his name is Ralph, and he says he'll be my friend. Can I keep him?"

"No, dear, you can't keep him. But he may be your friend and stay and play this afternoon. Now, go outside, and, please, no more questions about ANIMALS!"